For three big girls
and one LITTLE one—
Chloe, Julie, Maria,
and Ada

First U.S. edition 2020

Library of Congress Catalog Card Number 2020910707
ISBN 978-1-5362-0936-5

20 21 22 23 24 CCP 10 9 8 7 6 5 4 3 2

Printed in Shenzhen, Guangdong, China

This book was typeset in Gill Sans.
The illustrations were done in watercolor and ink.

Candlewick Press
99 Dover Street
Somerville, Massachusetts 02144

visit us at www.candlewick.com

CANDLEWICK PRESS

SOME DINOSAURS are SMALL

CHARLOTTE VOAKE

Some dinosaurs
are small.

They have
tiny flat teeth
for munching
through
fruit and
leaves.

Some
dinosaurs
are
BIG.

They have
huge pointy
teeth
and sharp
claws.

They are always
thinking about their
next meal . . .

and they can run
like the wind!

They take food
from little
dinosaurs,

and when they've
finished eating it,
they go looking
for more!

But . . .

while some dinosaurs are BIG,
with huge pointy teeth and sharp claws,

and some dinosaurs are small, with tiny flat teeth for munching through fruit and leaves . . .

some dinosaurs . . .

are **simply** . . .

ENOR